"CHICKEN SOUP for LITTLE SOULS.

"The New Kid and the Cookie Thief"

Story Adapted from
"The Cookie Thief"
by Valerie Cox

Story Adaptation by
Lisa McCourt

Illustrated by
Mary O'Keefe Young

Health Communications, Inc.
Deerfield Beach, Florida

Library of Congress Cataloging-in-Publication Data

McCourt, Lisa.
    Chicken soup for little souls : the new kid and the cookie thief / story adapted by Lisa McCourt ;
illustrated by Mary O'Keefe Young.
       p. cm.
    "Inspired by . . . 'Chicken soup for the soul' by Jack Canfield and Mark Victor Hansen."
    Summary: Nervous and shy about being the new kid on the first day of school, Julie has a rough start
trying to make friends, but things get better as the day goes on.
    ISBN 1-55874-588-2
    [1. Bashfulness—Fiction. 2. Friendship—Fiction. 3. Schools—Fiction.]
    I. Young, Mary O'Keefe, ill. II. Title.
    PZ7.M47841445Cg   1998
    [E]—dc21

                                           98-5111
                                            CIP
                                            AC

©1998 Health Communications, Inc.
ISBN 1-55874-588-2

Story adapted from "The Cookie Thief" by Valerie Cox, *A 3rd Serving of Chicken Soup for the Soul®*, edited by Jack
Canfield and Mark Victor Hansen.

Story Adaptation ©1998 Lisa McCourt
Illustrations ©1998 Mary O'Keefe Young

Cover Design by Cheryl Nathan

Produced by Boingo Books, Inc.

Publisher: Health Communications, Inc.
               3201 S.W. 15th Street
               Deerfield Beach, FL 33442-8190

Printed in Mexico

The new kid, I thought, hating the sound of it. *That's what I'll be today. Everyone will notice me. Everyone will know I don't belong.*

I wished for the hundredth time that I weren't so shy. Talking to new people was always hard for me. Especially a whole new school full of kids. My stomach hurt just thinking about it.

My big sister, Jen, tried to cheer me up. "Here, Julie," she said. "Take this bag of Choco-Bites to school today. At lunch time you can share them with the other kids. It'll help you meet them."

Choco-Bites were the most popular, best cookies there were. Everybody loved them. But could they really help me make friends? "Thanks, Jen," I said. "But I don't think I'm brave enough to share these with complete strangers."

"That's the whole trick to making friends!" Jen said. "Don't wait for the other kids to be friendly. Be friendly first."

"I'll try," I promised her.

I was so nuts with worry all morning that I fed cat food to the dog, tried to put my shoes on the wrong feet, and almost forgot to brush my teeth. I walked the short block to the bus stop wondering what absent-minded thing I'd do next.

A boy about my age was sitting on the bus stop bench when I got there. He didn't say a word to me, so I pretended not to notice him. *He probably can tell I'm new*, I thought.

I sat on the bench and worried some more about my first day of school. What if no one talked to me all day? What if no one at this school ever liked me at all? I had been too nervous to eat breakfast, and now my tummy was rumbling.

To make myself feel better, I opened the bag of Choco-Bites beside me and ate a cookie. Then the boy on the bench reached into the bag and took a cookie, too. I thought about Jen's idea that sharing the cookies would help me make friends. Should I talk to the boy?

   While I was deciding what to say, the boy took three more cookies! He barely even looked at me as he took cookie after cookie from the bag and munched away. *How rude!* I thought. *He's not even saying "thank you." I'm not going to try to make friends with a cookie thief. If I weren't so shy, I'd tell him to get his own snack!*

   I decided that if he was going to eat up my whole bag of Choco-Bites, I might as well get some before they were gone.   So for every cookie he took, I took one, until just one cookie was left. The boy took it out and smiled at me. Then he broke it in half and popped half in his mouth while he handed the other half to me.

Just then, the bus pulled up. I stomped away from the bench without looking at the cookie thief and got on the bus. I sat by myself feeling worse than ever. Everyone around me seemed to know each other. They joked and laughed and whispered secrets until I felt the tears filling my eyes. A whole new school full of kids, and the first one I'd come across had eaten up my only chance for making friends. Some of the kids even said "hi" to the cookie thief as they boarded the bus. They called him "Brian."

When the bus stopped at the school, everyone ran off like they knew exactly where to go. I followed them, trying to be invisible. Finally, I found my classroom.

"I'm happy to meet you, Julie," said the teacher with a big, warm smile. Mr. Robinson had dark, curly hair and the kindest eyes I'd ever seen. When he talked to me, I felt like he knew just how scared I was and how hard it was to be the new kid.

When everyone was in their seats, Mr. Robinson said, "We have a new student today. Let's all welcome Julie and show her what a friendly class we are." I felt like a hundred unfamiliar eyes were staring at me. *Is there a friend anywhere here for me?* I wondered.

At least Mr. Robinson didn't make me tell the class about myself. He just led me to an empty desk by the window and gave me some books. I looked at the girl in the seat next to mine. She was wearing a fuzzy green sweater and she looked like she'd be nice. *Maybe she'll be my friend,* I thought.

Behind her was Brian, the cookie thief. He smiled at me when I noticed him, but I didn't smile back. Who wanted a rude boy like that for a friend?

When lunch hour finally came, I walked with my class to the lunchroom. The other kids all talked and laughed together. Just like I had suspected, I was alone.

I sat down and sadly opened my lunch box. I couldn't believe it—there was my bag of Choco-Bites! As soon as I saw them, I remembered putting them in my lunch box that morning. I had been so crazy with worry, I thought the cookies on the bus stop bench were mine...when really the cookies I had opened and eaten with Brian were *his cookies*!

That meant that Brian had done exactly what Jen had told me to do. He had been friendly first. *I* was the cookie thief and he had shared his cookies with me to be nice. How could I ever face him now?

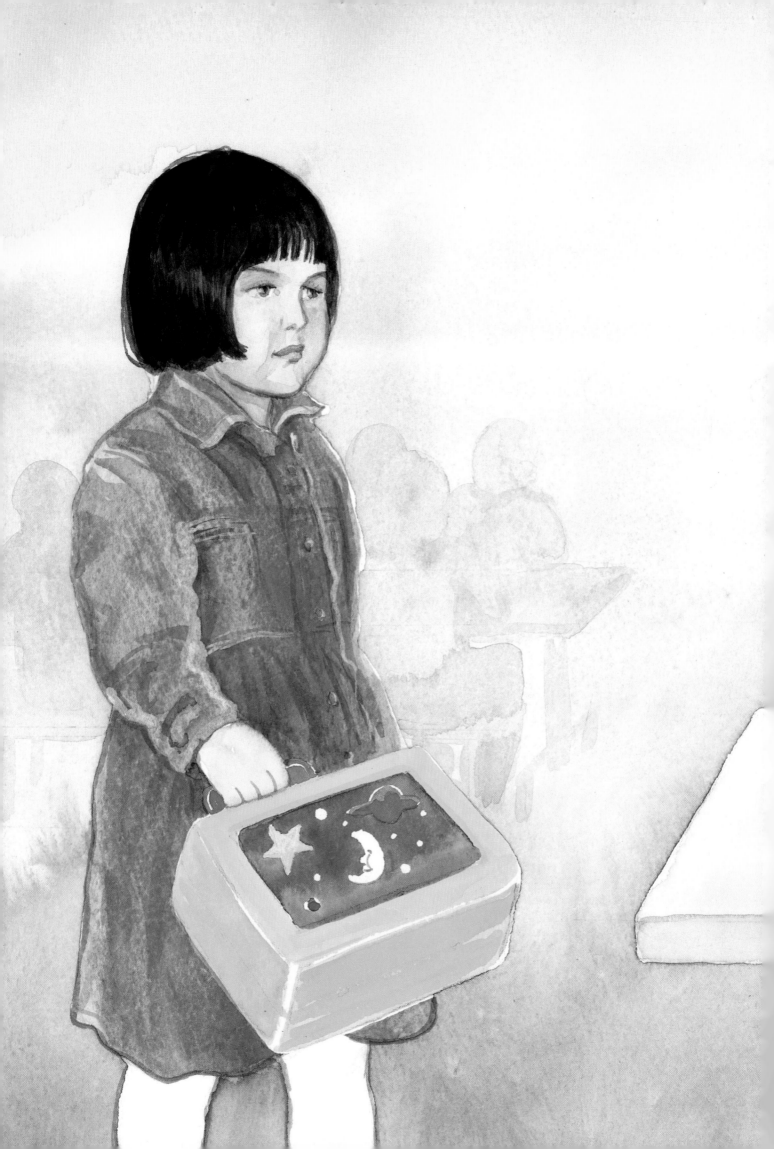

I looked around the lunch room. Brian was eating lunch with the girl in the green sweater. I knew I had to go tell him I was sorry, but it was such a scary thing to do for someone shy like me.

I picked up my lunch box and walked across the big lunch room to Brian's table. "Um...Brian," I said, swinging my lunch box nervously by my side.

He looked up just as I accidentally swung my lunch box right into the table with a loud crash. The clasp popped open and out spilled my whole lunch!

"Wow, you sure do like Choco-Bites," said Brian, seeing the full
bag on the floor with my peanut butter sandwich and carrot sticks.

I had never been so embarrassed, but I knew I had to finish what I'd come to do. "Brian, I'm sorry I ate your cookies without asking this morning. I thought that was my bag of Choco-Bites on the bench. I didn't even say 'thank you.' I feel terrible."

"That's okay," he said. "There was plenty to share."

He seemed so nice. Picking my lunch up off the floor, I took a deep breath and asked, "Can I eat lunch with you?"

"Sure," said Brian, sliding over to make room for me. "This is my friend, Ellen." He wasn't mad about the cookies! And no one even laughed at me for spilling my lunch box!

Ellen and Brian were both super. I told them all about my old school and the friends I had there, and they told me lots of neat things about my new school. I finally got to share my cookies, but I knew by then that the cookies really didn't matter. Brian and Ellen liked me just for me. And by the time lunch was over I had two new friends!

I couldn't believe how different the classroom felt as I filed back in with all the other kids. I was still shy, but I wasn't a stranger. I knew that I had made two friends and that I could make more.

It was just like Jen had said. All I had to do was be friendly first!